# Fascism Speaks
## Book 2

# Also from EATMS Productions

Nonfiction
Billionaires, Capitalism, and Power

Evil and the Mountain Ungreed
Self Help for American Billionaires
Selfish Steve and the Ivory Tower
Tariffs, Taxes, & Face-Eating Leopards
Ban Billionaires: Fascism Fix

Fascism, Religion, and Cultural Control

Self Help for the Manosphere
Fascism 2025
Fascism & the Perverts & the Greed Virus
Christian Fascism Marriage Book
Tyranny, Table Manners, & Tiramisu

Guides for Women's Autonomy and Protection

How to Survive in Post-America as a Woman
Project 2025 American Drag
4B – Burn, Ban, Boycott, Build
4B OG – So No Go GYN
I'm Glad He's Dead

Analysis of Authoritarian Project 2025

Project 2025: The Blueprint
Project 2025: The List
Project 2025, Christian Dumb Dumbs, & The Republican
Agenda
Fascism, Project 2025, & The Pinkprint

Modern Rewrites for Women

Stoic Principles Reimagined
Siddhartha Reimagined
The Prince Reimagined for Women
The Art of War Reimagined for Women
The Jungle Reimagined
The Constitution Reimagined for Women

Machine Learning Series

AI, Bitcoin, Nostr for Women
AI, Safety, & Security for Women
AI, Anxiety, & Health for Women
AI, Kids, & Family Safety for Women
AI, Creativity, & Personal Expression for Women
AI, Independent Work, & Parallel Power for Women

Social Systems Series

Emotional Labor for Women
Household Power for Women
Workplace Power for Women
Medical Bias for Women
Aging Systems for Women
Recovery Systems for Women

Fiction
Propaganda Paige & the Missing Prosperity
Propaganda Paige & the TIDE Manifesto
Propaganda Paige & the Shadow Cartographers
Propaganda Paige & the Prosperity Alliance
Propaganda Paige & the Shattered Truth
Propaganda Paige & the Rising TIDE
Propaganda Paige & the Last Bastion
Propaganda Paige & the Dawn of Prosperity
Project 2025: Dorian — The Last Men
Project 2025: Boy — A Last Men Novel

# Propaganda Paige & The TIDE Manifesto

## Fascism Speaks 2/8

by
Sable Moncrieff

**EATMS**
PRODUCTIONS

ISBN: 978-1-966014-20-1

Cover, interior design by: Esme Mees

eatms@pm.me
www.eatms.me

Check out EATMS Underground:
https://tinyurl.com/eatmsNOSTR

Printed in the United States of America.

*I do not study to know more, but to ignore less.*

— Sor Juana Inés de la Cruz

# Table of Contents

# Foreword

Fear built this country faster than faith ever could. Salem was its first cathedral, a rehearsal for the idea that weak men could turn their trembling into law. They wrapped their fear in scripture, nailed it to every door, and called it virtue. A woman's defiance was never the danger; it was her clarity.

The witch trials were not madness. They were management. Each accusation was a sermon disguised as justice, a way to keep the powerful steady by keeping everyone else afraid. Weak men love purity because it forgives their cruelty. They break what they do not understand and kneel before the pieces. When the smoke rises, they call it proof that God was listening.

Paige does not come to save anyone. She comes to interrupt the pattern. Her violence is revelation. In Salem she finds the same code that still runs through every pulpit and parliament: fear pretending to be faith, cowardice rewarded as order. The witch-burners demanded obedience. She offers reflection. And when they finally see themselves, the illusion of holiness collapses into something closer to truth.

"They call her witch.
They call her Devil.
They call her propaganda.

Paige calls it correction."

—Esme Mees, Fall 2025

# ~1
# Enter Salem

Salem, 1692. Night rain. Mud as deep as a memory you try to forget. Torches spit and crack. The gallows shines like a butcher block rubbed with fat. The square breathes heavy. Men laugh because laughter makes murder feel like chores. Women press in at the edges and hold their shawls tight. Boys climb rails and swear they are not scared. The preacher warms his voice with a psalm that sounds like a threat.

Paige steps out of the dark and into the crowd. Hood down. Face wet. Calm. She moves like she owns the ground. She does not rush. She chooses where every heel lands. She watches hands. She watches eyes. She watches the rope. She smells the oil on the musket stocks and the iron in new timber.

The condemned is a girl named Mary. She is small and already used up by work and by fear. Hands tied. Mouth set. She is not brave and she is not weak. She is human in a place that has no use for that word. The butcher tests the knot and nods like a craftsman. A teenage seer shakes beside the stairs, eyes rolled white for anyone who will look. He loves the sound of his own visions. He says a shape sits over the square. He keeps saying Mary's name wrong and it makes him smile.

The Reverend closes his eyes. He prays loud. "Purity will walk among us again." His voice swells like he has God by the throat. He does not speak of the boy he hurt or the woman he shamed or the coin pocketed after a whispered confession. He rubs a ring with a red stone and waits for the cheer. He wants fireworks out of fear.

Paige stands at the base of the platform and looks up. She counts the nails. She counts the men with blades. She notes the one with a limp and the one with a twitch in his finger. She notes the young guard who looks sick. She notes the old woman biting her tongue bloody to keep from screaming. She notes how the crowd hangs on the seer's voice like it is candy.

The cart rolls. The rope drops. The square tightens. Paige steps onto the first stair. A constable sees her. "Halt," he says. She looks at him. He chokes on the word and swallows it.

The Reverend lifts his hands. "Is there mercy in any soul here?"

A man shouts, "Mercy is for saints."

The seer moans and points at the sky. "A woman walks with a wolf," he cries. "The wind speaks. It says feed me."

Paige slides through the bodies, out the side where the boys grip the fence. One spits into the mud. Another whispers that he saw a witch turn into smoke once. Paige stops beside them. "Did you?" she asks. The boy grins like a stray dog. She smiles once, small and private. It fades like a match in rain.

The butcher slips the rope over Mary's head. The young guard looks away. The Reverend asks for last words. Mary says none. She wants the noise to stop. She wants the sky.

Paige moves.

Not fast. Right. She reaches the butcher from behind and touches his elbow. He turns. He sees a wet face and quiet eyes. She holds his look for a count. He decides she is nothing. He turns back.

She takes his knife.

No speech. No warning. She cuts deep behind his knee and keeps walking. He drops, blood and rain mixing in the boards. The crowd jolts. The seer keeps moaning. The Reverend keeps talking. The young guard fumbles his musket. Paige is already gone.

She climbs the second stair, draws the musket from the guard, and leans it against the post. He turns, confused. She puts two fingers to his throat, gentle, then presses until he sleeps. He sinks to his knees like prayer gone empty. She leaves him there.

The Reverend's voice rises. "We cleanse this town!"

Paige steps into the light. Everyone sees her.

She is not a witch. She is not a savior. She is a fact.

The Reverend stammers. The seer points and squeals, "Witch! Witch!"

Paige climbs the last stair. She faces Mary. Their faces are inches apart. Mary's eyes are wide and wet and angry. Paige tightens the knot by a hair. Mary gasps. Paige whispers, "Soon."

Paige turns to the crowd. She lifts both hands, palms open. "Proceed."

The Reverend finds his voice. "Purge the sin!"

Paige kicks the stool herself.

Mary drops. The rope snaps tight. The crowd gasps. The Reverend lifts the Bible and shouts blessed words like nails. Paige steps behind him, grabs his robe, and jerks him forward. Mary's body swings. His chin hits her heel. Teeth crack. Blood sprays. The Bible falls into the mud and drinks rain like holy wine.

The constable charges. Paige lifts the resting musket and breaks it across his face. Wood cracks. Bone gives. He goes down hard. Another man grabs for her coat. She drives an elbow into his throat. He drops to his knees clawing at air. The sleeping guard tries to stand. She pushes him back with her boot and he slides off the plank into the mud and stays there, coughing.

The seer lunges, all bones and noise. He claws for her hair. She catches his wrist, twists until the bone pops, and smashes his head into the post. Blood streaks down the wood like a red hymn. He slumps to his knees, eyes glassy. She lifts him by the hair until his feet barely find the boards.

"Tell them the truth," she says.

He gurgles. She slams him once more. "Say her name."

He gasps, "Mary."

"Louder."

"Mary."

The crowd murmurs it back, not a cheer, not a prayer. A low unsure echo as if the ground itself speaks through them. "Mary." The word pushes down alleys, through shutters, into rooms where women sit with lamps turned low. "Mary."

Paige steadies the body with her hands. One palm on Mary's calf. One on the skirt. The swing softens, stops. It is tender in a way that makes the crowd more afraid.

"This is your worship," she says. "This is your profit. You did not hang a witch. You hung a girl because a man told you to and a boy liked the attention."

The Reverend tries to shout blasphemy. It comes out a wet cough. He stares at his teeth in the mud as if faith might crawl back into his mouth.

A militia man shoves forward with a club. Paige leans inside the swing, breaks his elbow with a pop, steals the club, and puts it into a second man's temple. He drops, legs twitching. She drops the club. "I don't carry your tools," she says, and steps past them to the edge of the platform.

"Seize her," the Reverend spits. "Seize her now."

No one moves.

Something inside the square loosens and slumps. A woman starts to cry and does not cover her face. A boy climbs down from the rail and takes his brother's hand. The butcher whimpers where he sits, leg pouring red, hands slick, mouth praying to anything that will answer. The old woman who bit her tongue stops biting it. She lets the blood spill down her chin and stares at Paige like she is finally awake.

Paige walks to the back stairs and descends. She moves slow to let them all see. She circles the scaffold, climbs again from the rear, reaches above the knot, and cuts the rope clean. Mary's body drops into her arms like a child who has finally fallen asleep. Paige kneels and lays the girl in the mud as if the mud were a bed. She smooths the hair from Mary's face. She closes the eyes. She takes the rope, coils it into a neat loop, and tucks it into her coat.

A dog creeps from under a wagon. It sniffs the hem of Paige's coat and wags once. It pads to Mary's side and lies down, muzzle on the girl's wrist, waiting for a pulse that will not come. Paige touches the dog's head without looking.

The Reverend wobbles on his feet. He hauls the Bible up by its spine. Filth drips from the pages. He lifts it toward the crowd as if to bless them with mud. "This is the Lord's will," he rasps. "This is—"

"This is you," Paige says.

His mouth snaps shut.

Two more guards push through, younger, scared, all angles and duty. "Stand aside," one says. "Stand aside or we will fire."

"You won't," Paige says.

They raise muskets anyway. The pans hiss in the rain. The flints spark but the powder is wet. The loudest thing is their breathing. A man in the crowd laughs once and cannot stop. It turns into a sob.

Paige steps off the platform. The crowd parts for her like a curtain. Even those who hate her move away. Hate is not courage. Hate is habit.

She passes a woman with a baby bound to her chest. The baby watches her with steady eyes. The woman whispers, "Bless." Paige does not bless. She nods once and keeps moving.

A brave man lunges. He is brave and late. She sidesteps, catches his wrist, and drives his own knife into his thigh. He screams and staggers into a trough. He goes under and comes up coughing mud, knife lost, courage gone.

A third guard tries to be a hero and trips over the sleeping one. They spill together in the mud. A boy helps them up by instinct then snatches his hand back as if he touched fire. He stares at his palm like it will tell him what he is.

Paige stops at the edge of the square and turns one last time. She looks at the faces. She looks at the wet map of blood and rain that has already forgotten which is which. "Tomorrow," she says, "you will tell each other that God was here tonight. He was not. I was."

Silence holds for a count. Then the square exhales all at once. The sound is not relief. It is a new kind of fear that does not know its own name yet.

The Reverend rallies. Spit threads from his lip. "To the church," he croaks. "Rouse the bell. Bring chains. Bring fire." He points at Paige with a hand that shakes. "Find her."

No one runs. They drift, as if leaving a grave they dug for themselves. A few men drag the wounded. Women tear sleeves for bandages. The boys scatter like birds shot at with words. The dog does not move. It keeps its head on Mary's wrist.

Paige steps into the alley behind the tavern. Rain drums on the barrels. She dips her hands in a cask and watches the water go red, then pink, then clear. She feels the weight of the coiled rope against her ribs. She listens to the square try to sew itself back into a story and fail.

She looks up at the parsonage window. A candle moves. A woman's shape crosses the light and pauses. "Soon,"

Paige says to no one, to the rain, to the fold humming like a vein in the dark.

She slips along the church wall. Her palm finds the lock. She can feel where the key bites by the star-shaped scratch around the hole. She can see the groove worn in the sill by something heavy dragged through again and again. She knows there is a room behind this door where fear has been stored like grain. She does not smile. She does not need to.

Boots splash behind her. Two men whisper bravado into each other's ears. "She went this way." "You first." Paige steps back into shadow and lets them pass. They shoulder through the door to the vestry with a shout. The room beyond is dark. She hears one trip, one curse, the hollow sound of a skull against a pew. She closes the door and drops the bar on the outside. The wood thuds. The men pound. "Open," they bark. "In the Lord's name."

"In whose name?" Paige asks.

They do not answer. They do not know the right one.

She moves on.

At the far edge of the square, a bell rings once from nowhere. No one pulled the rope. The sound just happens, like breath. The torches gutter in a wind that has not arrived. Somewhere a cow lows in a field and answers itself. The world stands on the seam between what it was told and what it is.

By the time the Reverend finds his feet, Paige is gone. He looks at the scaffold and sees a body without a rope, a platform slick with blood, a crowd that will not look him in the eye. He lifts the Bible with both hands and tries to raise his voice. It breaks. The sound that comes out is small and human. He hates it.

The seer crawls to the edge of the platform and vomits into the mud. He whispers "Mary" into his own palm and weeps because the word feels heavier now. He will tell the story all night. He will tell it wrong and right and wrong again because fear is a megaphone that will use any mouth.

The square thins. Doors open and close. The rain slackens to a patient mist. The dog stays. It noses Mary's sleeve once more then tucks its nose under its paw. It makes a sound that might be grief or might be the noise a living thing makes when a story changes shape.

Paige cuts across the common to the black seam of trees. She listens. Far off, the river talks to stones. Closer, a child coughs. The fold hums under the skin of the world like an old machine waiting for a hand. She steps into the dark under the branches, soft and simple, like a knife slipping back into its sheath.

# ~2
# The Pastor and the Pot

The parsonage sits at the edge of the square like a wound that never closed. Its shutters are tight. Its walls sweat from the rain. The roof groans under the weight of a night that refuses to end. Inside, a single fire burns and makes the shadows dance.

Reverend Samuel Parris kneels by the hearth. His knees creak against the plank floor. His lips move around words older than the bones beneath him. The smell of stew fills the room, lamb, onion, a hint of copper. He calls it supper. His wife, Ruth, calls it endurance.

Ruth stirs the pot with a wooden spoon worn smooth as a prayer bead. Her hands are red from washing linen in lye. She hums a psalm under her breath but stops each time he glances over his shoulder. He likes quiet when he communes with God.

Outside, rain scrapes the windows. Paige stands under the eaves, hood low, watching the light pulse through the curtain. Smoke leaks through the cracks of the chimney. She watches the shadows stretch long and thin across the floorboards inside. She can smell sin through the mortar.

She taps the door once with her knuckles. A soft, hollow sound.

Ruth jumps. The spoon clatters against the pot. "Who's there?" she whispers.

Parris straightens, shoulders square. "At this hour?"

Paige's voice comes through the wood. Calm. "A traveler seeking rest."

Ruth hesitates. "Samuel, she sounds—"

He cuts her off. "The Devil knocks softest." He grips the poker and moves toward the door. The hinges whine as he pulls it open.

Paige stands framed in the rain, water running off her coat, hair stuck to her cheek. She looks young and eternal at the same time. "Good evening, Reverend."

"Who sent you?" he demands.

"The storm," she says.

Ruth steps forward. "Let her in. The fire's warm."

Parris hesitates, then nods, as if generosity were a performance for an unseen judge. "A moment, no more."

Paige steps inside. Heat hits her like a breath. The room smells of smoke and boiled bone. She closes the door behind her and stands silent. Rain slides off her coat and pools at her boots.

Parris watches her like a snake deciding whether to strike. "You are soaked," he says.

"Rain does that," Paige answers.

His lips press tight. "Your tone borders on insolence."

"So does hunger," she says, looking toward the pot.

Ruth bites back a smile. "Sit," she says softly. "You can dry by the fire."

Paige sits on the floorboards near the flames. The heat paints her face gold. For a moment she looks almost human, but her eyes remain sharp, reflective, unyielding.

Parris sits at the table and bows his head. "Lord, grant us discernment against false spirits and temptresses who walk in shadow."

Paige murmurs, "Maybe start with yourself."

His head jerks up. "What did you say?"

"Just thinking aloud," she says, calm.

Ruth sets the table, careful not to make noise. She places a bowl before him and one for herself. None for Paige.

He eats slowly, savoring each bite as if chewing proof of divine favor. "The trials will resume at dawn," he says between mouthfuls. "Three more witches to hang before the Sabbath."

Paige watches him eat. "And after that?"

"After that, peace," he says. "When sin is purged, peace follows."

Ruth speaks quietly. "Peace never stays."

Parris slams his spoon against the bowl. "You forget your place."

"I remember it every day," she says.

Paige looks at Ruth. "Does he hit you?"

Ruth flinches. Parris stands so fast his chair skids back. "You speak blasphemy under my roof!"

Paige rises. "You don't own this roof."

"I own this house," he snarls. "I own what's in it."

"You own nothing," Paige says. "You borrow fear and call it faith."

He raises his hand. She doesn't move. He swings, but her hand catches his wrist mid-air. The bones in his arm crack. The poker falls from his grip.

Ruth gasps. "Stop! Please."

Paige turns her head slightly. "He should stop first."

Parris tries to pull free. "The Lord will judge you!"

"He already did," Paige says. "He sent me."

He lunges again. She twists his arm until the joint pops. His knees buckle. She drags him forward and slams his head against the edge of the table. Wood splinters. His breath leaves in a grunt.

"Sit," she says. He collapses onto the chair, gasping.

Ruth moves to him. Paige lifts a hand. "No. Let him hear."

Parris wheezes. "You're a witch."

Paige kneels beside him. "You call every woman a witch when she doesn't kneel low enough. The word has lost its teeth."

He spits blood onto the floor. "You will hang."

"Maybe. But not tonight." She glances at the pot simmering on the fire. "What's in there?"

"Stew," Ruth whispers.

Paige walks to it. The steam hits her face. She smells meat, salt, something darker. "You put fear into everything you cook," she says. "Even your food begs forgiveness."

Parris drags himself toward her. "Step away from my hearth."

She grips the iron handle and tips the pot forward until the stew hisses onto the coals. The flames flare, casting his face in trembling red light. "I am," she says.

He screams, lunging. She sidesteps, catches him by the hair, and forces his face toward the boiling rim. He thrashes, but she's stronger. The air fills with the smell of sweat and scald. His cries turn to choked gurgles.

"Repent," Paige says.

Ruth covers her mouth, tears streaming. "Please stop."

Paige eases the Reverend back. His face shines, half blistered, half wet. He collapses to his knees, shaking.

"You'll burn," he gasps.

"You already are," Paige says.

She looks at Ruth. "Do you want him dead?"

Ruth shakes her head violently. "No. I just want quiet."

"Then you'll need to leave," Paige says. "He'll never stop talking."

Ruth's voice is small. "He says if I leave, I'll die in sin."

Paige smiles faintly. "Then die free."

She steps over the Reverend's sprawled form and crouches beside him. "Listen carefully," she says.

"When they ask what happened here, you will tell them the Devil came to dinner. And she ate your pride."

He moans, clutching at his scorched cheek.

Paige picks up his ring from the floor. The ruby catches the firelight. "This stone cost a woman her house," she says. "Maybe her child." She sets it on the table. "You should give it back."

She turns to Ruth. "When he sleeps, take his horse. Ride west. Don't stop until you forget his name."

Ruth nods through tears. "Who are you?"

Paige looks toward the fire. "A correction."

Thunder rolls outside. The walls tremble.

Parris crawls toward the Bible on the mantel. He opens it with burned fingers and tries to read, but the letters swim. He weeps. "God help me."

Paige's voice is steady. "He tried. You talked over Him."

She walks to the door. The wind forces it open before she touches the latch. Rain slants in sideways.

Ruth whispers, "He'll call for you. He'll say you're the Devil."

Paige glances back. "Let him. It's the first true thing he'll ever preach."

She steps into the storm. The wind catches her coat and makes it billow like wings. The thunder swallows her shape.

Inside, Ruth kneels by her husband. She touches his face with trembling fingers. "Samuel," she whispers, "look at me."

He turns his head. His skin peels in strips. He breathes through clenched teeth. "She was evil."

Ruth shakes her head. "No. She was right."

She looks at the spilled stew, the scorched wood, the ring gleaming on the table. She takes it and drops it into the fire. The ruby melts first.

Parris howls, crawling toward the flames. "No! My mark of covenant!"

Ruth stands. "Your covenant is broken."

Outside, Paige walks past the church. The bell rope sways in the wind though no one pulls it. Smoke rises from the chimney and joins the rain.

She stops at the graveyard fence. Her reflection shimmers in a puddle, blurred by ripples. The air hums with the low vibration of the fold. The horizon bends slightly, like fabric pulled by invisible hands.

She says quietly, "He was not here tonight."

Lightning answers. Then she is gone.

# ~3
# The Girls Who Point

Morning drags itself across Salem like a hungover preacher. The storm is gone, but the mud stays. Smoke still crawls from the scaffold ruins. Every doorway smells of ash and gossip. The town has not slept. They whisper about the woman who cut down the witch. They call her ghost, sinner, saint, nightmare. They can't decide which name frightens them more.

In the meetinghouse yard, a group of girls gathers near the well. They are the "afflicted," the holy daughters, the trembling choir that points and convulses and makes men righteous. Their dresses cling wet to their knees. They talk in low, excited tones about the hanging that failed to stay neat. About the stranger who stepped out of the rain.

Abigail, the oldest, holds a crucifix like a weapon. She is seventeen and already half-famous. People bring her ribbons and fruit, hoping to be spared her visions. Mercy Lewis leans against the well, combing her hair with her fingers. Her nails are bitten to the quick. She says the Devil's hand touched her shoulder last night. Ann Putnam laughs and says maybe it just wanted company.

Paige stands behind the fence, hood down, watching them through the slats. Her hands rest on the rough wood. She listens. The girls sound like sparrows trying to out-scream the wind.

Abigail says, "The Reverend said she was the Devil herself."

Mercy answers, "Then why didn't the ground open?"

"Because," Abigail says, "she's not finished."

The others nod. They like the story better when it's not over.

Paige steps through the gate. The hinges cry. The girls turn, all eyes at once, startled then curious. She walks slowly toward them, mud sucking at her boots.

"Who are you?" Abigail asks, voice high, performative.

"No one," Paige says. "And you?"

Abigail lifts her chin. "We are the chosen. We see what others can't."

Paige studies her face. "You see everything except yourselves."

Mercy smirks. "You talk like a preacher."

"Only when I'm bored," Paige says.

The circle tightens. The girls glance at one another, emboldened by numbers. The youngest, Sarah, whispers, "She's the one they spoke of. The witch who saved the witch."

Abigail takes a step forward. "If you are innocent, you will not fear God's test."

"I don't fear God," Paige says. "He's quiet."

The older girl's smile hardens. "Then the Devil speaks for you."

Paige shrugs. "Maybe he listens better."

The girls gasp. Abigail drops to her knees and begins to shake. "She mocks the Lord!" she screams. Her body jerks. Foam gathers at her mouth. The others join her, thrashing, shrieking, hands clawing at the air.

Paige watches, expressionless. She waits for the performance to crest. Then she begins to move.

She mimics their convulsions, step for step, sound for sound. Her body snaps backward, her head jerks, her voice joins theirs. The rhythm syncs. To the onlookers who've begun to gather, a few merchants, a guard, a pair of wives, it looks like a contagion. Six girls writhing in the dirt, then seven.

Abigail opens her eyes mid-fit and sees Paige's face twisted into the same false agony. The mirror shocks her. She falters.

Paige keeps going. "It burns!" she cries. "It burns like purity!"

The crowd gasps.

Mercy points at her. "Witch!"

Paige points back. "Witch!"

The echo is exact. The sound hits like thunder. The crowd murmurs. Which one?

Paige rises to her feet, breathing hard, eyes blazing. "You call down judgment," she says, "but you don't even know what it costs."

Abigail stumbles upright. "We serve the Lord!"

"No," Paige says. "You serve applause."

The girls look to each other for a cue. None comes. Their unity cracks.

Paige steps closer to Abigail until their noses nearly touch. "When you screamed yesterday," she says softly, "what did you feel?"

Abigail's lip trembles. "The Devil's hand."

"No," Paige says. "You felt power. You felt the town look at you and tremble. And you liked it."

Abigail's hand twitches around the crucifix. "You lie."

Paige turns to the crowd. "They call this proof," she says. "They call their fits the Lord's truth. Watch closely."

She spreads her arms wide. "Go on," she says to the girls. "Show them your demons."

The girls hesitate. Mercy fakes a shiver but it looks rehearsed. Ann bites her lip. Sarah looks like she might cry.

Abigail breaks first. She screams and falls to her knees, shaking violently. The others join in. Paige waits a moment, then begins to mimic them again perfectly.

The crowd murmurs louder. Someone says, "It's in them both." Another whispers, "Which one started it?"

Paige stops mid-spasm and stands tall. The girls keep writhing.

"Tell me, Reverend," Paige calls to a man watching near the gate, "if both tremble, which one is guilty?"

The man stammers. "The one who confesses."

Paige smiles. "Then watch."

She kneels beside Abigail, who's still thrashing, and grips her jaw. "Confess," she whispers.

Abigail shakes her head, teeth chattering. "I—I see him! He stands beside you!"

Paige leans closer. "You see yourself."

She holds up the crucifix Abigail dropped. "This is not armor. It's a prop."

Abigail's eyes dart side to side. "You'll damn us all."

Paige says, "You already did."

She stands and turns to the crowd. "These girls learned from their fathers that fear can buy power. They learned it well. But they forgot that power bites."

A stone flies from the back of the crowd. It hits the well with a clang. Someone shouts, "Witch!"

Paige looks at the man who threw it. "The Devil's favorite word," she says.

Another stone flies, this one closer. The girls scatter behind the well, crying. Abigail scrambles to her feet. "Seize her!" she screams.

Paige doesn't run. She walks toward the man with the stones. "You think I'm the Devil?" she says.

He grips his next rock tighter. "You mock the Lord."

She nods. "So does He."

She closes the distance before he can throw. Her hand snaps up, catches his wrist. The stone drops. "You should save your strength," she says. "You'll need it." She twists. His arm cracks at the elbow. He screams and falls to his knees.

The crowd lurches back.

Abigail points, shaking. "She cursed him!"

Paige points at her. "No. You did."

Abigail freezes.

"Your voice made this," Paige says. "You call it holy, but it's just hunger with a hymn."

She looks at the other girls. "Go home," she says. "Wash your hands. They smell of ash."

They don't move.

The town constable pushes through the crowd, musket in hand. His face is pale, his boots splattered with last night's mud. "In the name of the court," he says, "you are under arrest for witchcraft."

Paige tilts her head. "Good. I've been looking for your court."

He raises the musket. "Stay where you are."

She steps forward. "Do you believe in what you're doing?"

He hesitates. "It isn't for me to believe."

"Then it's not justice," Paige says.

He cocks the hammer. The sound clicks through the yard like a curse.

Abigail screams, "Shoot her!"

Paige moves before the echo fades. She lunges, grabs the barrel, and shoves it upward. The gun fires into the sky. The recoil knocks the constable off his feet. Smoke rolls across the yard.

Paige pulls the weapon from his hands and points it at the ground between them. "This," she says, "is what faith looks like when you carve it from fear." She tosses it into the mud.

Abigail stares, shaking. "She cannot be human."

Paige says, "Neither can you."

She walks to the well and dips her hands into the water. Steam rises where her skin meets the surface, not from magic, but from heat and anger. She wipes her face and looks at the reflection rippling in the bucket. For a moment she sees two of herself, one made of flesh, one made of smoke.

When she turns, the girls are huddled together. Mercy is crying openly now. Sarah whispers, "I want to go home."

Paige nods toward the road. "Then go."

They look at Abigail. She glares at Paige but her voice breaks. "You'll burn."

Paige says, "Everyone does."

The girls flee, skirts snapping against their legs. The crowd parts for them. No one follows Paige. No one dares.

The constable groans from the ground. Paige kneels beside him and presses two fingers to his throat. "You're alive," she says. "That's your punishment."

He spits mud. "You'll hang."

Paige smiles faintly. "I'm patient."

She stands and looks toward the church spire in the distance. Bells begin to toll though no hands pull the ropes. The sound travels over the town like warning.

In the yard, Abigail has stopped at the corner. She looks back. Her face is pale, eyes wide, something dawning there, recognition or guilt. Paige raises a hand. Not to threaten. To bless. The gesture confuses everyone who sees it.

Abigail mouths something. Maybe a curse. Maybe a prayer. Then she runs.

Paige stays by the well until the yard empties. The water settles. The reflection clears. She sees Mary's face under the surface, the girl from the gallows, eyes open, hair floating like weeds. Paige doesn't flinch. "Rest," she says quietly. The reflection fades.

She hears footsteps behind her. Ruth Parris. The pastor's wife. Her dress is damp, her hands shaking. "He's alive," Ruth says. "He prays louder than before."

Paige doesn't turn. "He'll burn himself out."

Ruth swallows hard. "They'll come for you. The magistrates. Cotton Mather rides tomorrow."

"Good," Paige says.

Ruth steps closer. "What are you?"

Paige turns now. "Correction."

Ruth stares, breath short. "Why do you stay?"

"Because they keep lighting fires," Paige says. "Someone has to watch."

Ruth nods slowly. "If they catch you—"

"They won't," Paige says. "They'll catch themselves."

Ruth looks at the well. "They'll blame us all."

"They already do," Paige says. "That's what keeps them righteous."

The church bell tolls again, slower now, heavier. Paige lifts her eyes to the steeple cutting the gray sky. "Do you know what happens when a lie gets tired?" she asks.

Ruth shakes her head.

"It starts telling the truth."

She walks past Ruth toward the road. The mud sucks at her boots. The wind rises again, carrying the faint smell of burning pitch from the scaffold ruins. She stops at the gate and glances back. Ruth stands by the well, staring into the water.

"Tell them," Paige says.

"Tell them what?"

"The truth," Paige says. "They'll think it's witchcraft."

Then she's gone.

The town will call it a riot. The ministers will call it possession. The girls will call it a nightmare that doesn't end when they wake. But by dusk, word spreads: the afflicted have seen their own devils and lived. And somewhere, in a house with boarded windows, Reverend Parris hears about it and smiles through cracked lips. He whispers, "The Devil walks in a woman's skin."

And Paige, far down the road, hears him without hearing him. She answers the dark aloud. "I walk in my own."

The wind carries her voice through the trees, through the spire, through the sleeping town that dreams of purity and wakes to mirrors. Tomorrow they will hang three more witches. Tomorrow she will be waiting.

# ~4
# The Midnight Hunt

The woods around Salem are blacker than any sermon.
The trees drip with rain. Branches twist like fingers
trying to catch a secret. Somewhere ahead, dogs howl.
The sound rolls through the wet dark, echoing off bark
and bone.

Paige moves without hurry. Her coat hangs heavy, still
stained with the Reverend's blood and the butcher's.
The air smells of rot, smoke, and gunpowder. Behind
her, the town burns small fires in the mud, pyres for
reputation.

They started the hunt at midnight. The Reverend's face
wrapped in bandages, voice a rasp, pointed from the
pulpit and named her. "The witch who speaks like
scripture. The Devil's mouthpiece."

By dawn, the name had changed: Propaganda Paige.

They whispered it as warning, then as prayer. Children
said it in bed to keep nightmares polite. Soldiers carved
it into their bullets.

She heard them shouting it from the square as they
loaded muskets. "For God and for purity! Find her and
burn her!"

Now the shouts bleed through the forest. Torches bob
between trees. Lantern light trembles like fear

pretending to be brave. Paige can feel them out there, twenty men, maybe more, drunk on righteousness and the echo of their own names.

She crouches near a stream. The water is dark with ash runoff from the last fire. She dips her fingers, smears the black across her face, and whispers to herself, "Let them see what they made."

A musket cracks in the distance. The shot hits bark near her shoulder. She doesn't flinch.

"Move, witch!" a voice calls.

She straightens. "You're the first to speak truth tonight."

The woods answer with gunfire. Smoke crawls between trunks. Dogs bark, then whine. One yelps short and goes silent.

Paige steps out into the open path. She holds no weapon. Only the coiled rope she took from Mary's hanging. She twirls it once, loose and quiet. The end whispers through the air like memory.

The first man bursts from the undergrowth, torch in hand. His face is red with rain and fury. "Down!" he shouts, leveling his musket.

Paige moves before the spark. She grabs the barrel, slams it upward. The blast tears through the treetops. She steps inside his reach and drives her forehead into his mouth. Teeth break. He screams, drops the weapon.

She snatches it and fires into his chest. The recoil rocks her shoulder. He falls back into the mud, torch landing beside him. The flame eats his sleeve first, then his hair.

Another man rushes in. She swings the musket like an axe. It cracks his skull. He collapses face-first into the burning mud. The smell of cooking flesh joins the storm.

Three more. They hesitate, watching her silhouette framed by the fire. One whispers, "That's her. That's Paige."

She smiles. "It's late for introductions."

They fire together. She dives low, rolls through the mud, comes up behind a fallen tree. Splinters slice her cheek. She pulls a pistol from the dead man's belt, checks the powder, still dry.

She waits until they reload. She can hear the scrape of metal, the curse under breath. She fires once. A head snaps back, body jerks like a puppet cut from its string. The second man drops his weapon and runs. The third freezes, hands shaking.

Paige stands and walks toward him. "You want to live?"

He nods.

"Then tell them what you saw."

"What do I say?" he stammers.

"Say the truth," she says. "That God sent me to remind them He's tired of spectators."

She lets him go. He runs blind through the dark. The woods swallow him with a sound like teeth closing.

Another shout: "Circle left! Don't let her vanish!"

Lanterns swing through the branches. Muskets gleam. The men spread out in a crescent, boots sucking into mud.

Paige drags the rope through her hands, feeling its slickness, its history. She loops it over a low branch. She waits.

The first soldier stumbles into the clearing. His torch lights her face for an instant. He opens his mouth to scream. She swings the rope, hooks it around his throat, yanks hard. The branch bends, creaks. His heels scrape bark. She holds the line steady until his twitching stops. The rope hums.

"Paige!" another voice roars. "Show yourself!"

She steps into the open. "Here."

The musket flash lights her chest. She moves, but the ball grazes her shoulder. Heat blooms, wet and warm. She doesn't look down. She runs forward, hits him full-body, drives him against a tree. The barrel jams between his ribs. She shoves until the wood cracks. He gurgles, eyes wide.

Behind her, another man rushes in swinging a blade. She spins, catches his wrist, snaps it sideways. The knife falls. She catches it midair, buries it in his stomach. He gasps. She twists. "Confess," she whispers.

He chokes out, "I...serve..."

"You serve fear," she says, and pushes the blade up under his ribs. His body shudders once and goes slack.

The forest is a chorus of breath and rain. The living don't move. The dead steam.

Paige leans against the tree, blood seeping down her sleeve. She closes her eyes for a moment. The fold hums faintly, a pulse behind the world, restless, waiting. But she isn't done.

The dogs bark again, three this time. Closer. She hears the handlers shouting, "Drive her out!"

Paige kneels, dips her fingers in the mud, and draws a line across her throat. "Come on, then."

The first dog bursts through the brush, white teeth flashing. She sidesteps, catches its collar, and twists. The crack is quick. The second leaps. She grabs the musket from the ground, shoves the barrel down its throat, and fires. The shot blows the back of its head open. The third dog skids to a halt, whines, then runs.

The handlers stop when they see the smoke. One falls to his knees, muttering scripture. The other raises a torch like a cross. "Unclean thing!" he shouts.

Paige walks toward him. "That's what they called you when you were born," she says.

He stares, confused. She takes his torch, presses it against his coat. The fire catches. He screams, tries to beat it out. She holds him by the chin, forcing him to look at her. "See?" she says. "You're baptized now."

He collapses in the mud, flame licking his boots. The other handler runs.

Paige turns in a slow circle, surveying the clearing. Six bodies lie sprawled. Smoke from torches curls into the wet night. The air hums with iron.

A horn sounds in the distance, the magistrate's call. More coming. Maybe a dozen. She wipes her hands on her coat, leaves streaks like war paint. She takes one of the torches, walks to the edge of the clearing, and presses it against a hanging shroud of moss. The flame climbs the tree, leaps to another. The forest catches.

By the time the next wave of men arrives, the world is burning.

They stumble through smoke, coughing, eyes red. They see shadows moving between the trunks, too fast, too many. Paige's voice echoes from everywhere and nowhere.

"You called me witch. You called me whore. You called me Devil. I called you predictable."

One man shouts, "Face us!"

She does. Steps out from behind the smoke, eyes shining. "I'm right here."

They fire wild. Sparks jump, powder flashes. One shot grazes her leg, another tears through her sleeve. She keeps walking.

A man screams as a flaming branch falls. Another's coat ignites. Panic spreads faster than the fire. Muskets drop. Men run. The forest becomes a trap of smoke and heat.

Paige grabs one fleeing soldier, spins him around, and drives her knee into his stomach. He falls. She kneels over him. "Tell me," she says, "what sermon made you this stupid?"

He sobs. "I just—I followed orders."

She presses her hand to his throat. "That's what they all say." She squeezes until the breath stops.

The clearing glows red now. Embers float like prayers too light to reach heaven.

Paige steps into the center of it, coat torn, blood streaked, hair wet with rain and sweat. She lifts the rope again, throws it over another branch, and ties it to the broken musket stock.

"Propaganda Paige," someone whispers behind her, half in awe, half in horror.

She turns toward the voice. "That's new," she says.

The man lifts his weapon with shaking hands. "They say you speak words that turn men against God."

Paige walks closer until the barrel touches her chest. "Maybe I just remind them who God works for."

He fires. The click is dry, no powder. She takes the musket, spins it, cracks it across his jaw. Teeth fly. He falls face-first into the mud.

She looks down at him, voice low. "You wanted spectacle. This is it."

The fire climbs higher, lighting her from below. The trees scream as they split. She throws her rope into the flames. It burns bright, the smoke rising like a signal.

From the town below, the people can see the glow in the woods. They say it looks like a demon's crown. The Reverend tells them it's a sign. The magistrate calls it proof. The wives whisper it's justice.

By dawn, half the hunting party is missing. The survivors stagger back, clothes singed, eyes wide. They tell of a woman in the fire who walked through bullets and called the trees by name. They say her words crawled under their skin. They say the forest itself turned on them.

And by morning, Salem has a new sermon.

"Propaganda Paige," they say, "the witch who burns without smoke."

Children carve her name into fence posts. Wives whisper it before sleep. The men drink harder.

In the parsonage, Reverend Parris sits in the dark, face bandaged, voice a cracked whisper. "She speaks through mirrors," he says. "She makes truth sound holy."

His wife, Ruth, listens from the doorway. She does not correct him. She remembers the pot, the burns, the smell of his own flesh. She remembers the woman who told her to run.

In the woods, the fire burns out by sunrise. Ash covers the clearing. Birds return slow, cautious. Paige stands in the middle, surrounded by smoke and ruin. Her coat is torn open at the shoulder, blood drying dark.

She kneels, presses her palm into the wet earth, and leaves a print blackened with soot. The shape looks like a sigil. She whispers to the ground, "Write that down."

Then she rises, limps toward the river, and disappears into the mist.

Behind her, a crow lands on a branch and croaks three times. The sound carries to the town and dies there, swallowed by bells.

By evening, a new story has already begun to grow teeth. They say she is not one woman but many. That her words spread like plague. That she turns men's prayers into confessions.

They call her witch.
They call her Devil.
They call her propaganda.

Paige calls it correction.

# ~5
# The TIDE Manifesto

Night wet and low presses on the town like a lid. Ash still hangs in the eaves from the fires in the woods. Salem breathes in smoke and exhales rumor. The magistrates meet in a circle of candles and courage that smells like old coin. They call it counsel. It is a planning room for punishment.

Paige moves through alleys like a rumor. Her boots slap soft on boards slick with mud and blood. The name follows her now — Propaganda Paige — spat from mouths that want the story small and sharp. They try to put her in a headline so they can sleep. She lets them. Names are cheap. Truth is heavier.

The meetinghouse is a building that remembers voices. The rafters hold more prayer than wood. Tonight those rafters are full of men with maps and lists, with thick palms that never learned the shape of a child's hand. They speak of order and duty and how far a rope must hang to teach a lesson. Cotton Mather's name flickers at the edges of the plan, a scholar's consolation passed down like a cud.

Paige has watched them from windows, from gutters, from the hollow between two chimneys. She knows their habits: the way they pause for devil-light, the way they sharpen knives in prayer. She knows the route the constable will take home with his pocket heavy. She knows where they keep their keys, and where a man thinks his voice is private.

Tonight she does not come to watch. She comes to change the margins of their maps.

She slips through the side door of the meetinghouse while the men drink the comfort of each other's outrage. The candles throw their long, blunt shadows. The hymn books on the bench are closed like fangs. Paige moves without rustle. Her hand brushes the wood; she tastes the memory of sermons.

Beneath the pulpit, in a crawlspace the men call storage, she finds what she is not looking for and exactly what she needs. Tucked in a hollow in the joists, folded in oilcloth, is a slip of paper bound with twine and a small iron pin. The paper is older than the men in the room. The ink smells faintly of camphor and resolve. The letters are cramped, not the polished script of the learned, but the harsh block of someone who writes to be read quickly and obeyed faster.

She unfolds it with hands that do not tremble. The header is blunt: T.I.D.E. — The Theocratic Inversion Doctrine Experiment.

It is not a sermon. It reads like instruction. It is a discipline, an experiment in mirror and muscle. It says, in the precise voice of revolt: test the judges as they test others. Name the accuser. Answer accusation with its own grammar. When the town calls for spectacle, give spectacle back and make the spectacle ask itself for forgiveness. Use the rhythm of prayer to break the cadence of power.

Paige smiles, the expression of someone who has been studying a problem and found its answer in a margin. This is beautiful and terrible and useful. She tucks the paper into her coat against her heart. The fold hums along her spine like a string pulled tight.

Behind the pulpit, through the thin slat of a shutter, the magistrates are still arguing. One of them, a captain who likes to spit scripture between commands, rises and murmurs about making an example. "We will show them," he says, "what law looks like."

Paige thinks: good. The experiment needs examples.

She slips out and slides over roofs to the inn where the captain sleeps with his boots on and his conscience buried under rum. Men like him keep knives under mattresses and prayers in their pockets. She enters quiet, silent as smoke. The room smells of ale, and a ledger left open like an accusation. She has promised no ledgers, but men keep lists in their heads and scars in their locks.

The captain stirs, a hand to his throat for the muscle gone wrong. Paige moves like a surgeon and like a reaper in the same breath. Her blade speaks a sentence across the side of his neck. He wakes to blood and pain and the sudden betrayal of his own skin. He tries to call, mouth filling with the taste of iron. She finishes the sentence with a twist and a small, clean motion. He flops, a heap of cloth and regret. She wipes the blade with the sleeve of his coat and leaves it on the pillow where he used to place his hand to pray.

She does not go for trophies. She goes for change. If terror is taught, terror can be unlearned by its teachers.

By the time she returns to the square, the magistrates are shouting. Someone has found the captain and his face is pale like paper. Men run like dogs circling an unknown wound. They call for order and for God and for horsemen. Cotton Mather rides at dawn because scholars like to be present when things become historic.

Paige uses the TIDE instructions like a new map. They are small acts- simple inversions, and each inversion is a stone thrown into the town's glass pond. She begins with the constables because constables are the arteries of punishment. A rope here, a jammed lock there, a blade slipped into a boot. She is careful to make sound elsewhere: sudden screams that draw guards away, a false alarm of smoke on the far side of town. Men move to the noise and leave their posts. She takes advantage of the absences.

When a squad of three drunken constables loose themselves with curses and muskets, she is waiting in the narrow lane behind the tannery. One reaches for a bottle. Paige steps forward like a warning. She lurches into him and they collide; his elbow cracks on the stone. She seizes the musket, fires once into the mud at their feet to make them jump, then drives the butt into the jaw of the second. The third tries to run. She catches his ankle with a lash of rope and tumbles him into a heap. By the time the clamor draws neighbors to the windows, two men are out cold and one has a split lip that will mark his face as long as he lives.

The experiment requires performance. Fear rehearses its lines until they sound like truth. Paige writes a new script quick and loud. She sits on the back of a cart in the center of town with the captain's coat flung over her knees like a proclamation. She pulls the TIDE slip from inside her breast and nails it to a post with a shard of metal, the letters black against the rain-matted wood.

She reads aloud, and her voice is a bell. "The Theocratic Inversion Doctrine Experiment," she says. "If your law claims holiness because it kills, then let the judges feel the gallows they raise."

The people hush because they always listen when a sermon arrives, even if the sermon is not from a pulpit they recognize. Paige reads the lines and makes them call-and-response. "If they name the witch, name the judge," she intones. "If they demand spectacle, demand their confession. If they build a scaffold, weigh it with their own names."

A man in the crowd spits. "She's a witch," he says, and then flinches because the words are not the same when the cadence is reversed. Someone else in the crowd mutters about blasphemy. The constables watch, uncertain, as if they have been given the wrong script.

Paige does not let the moment cool. She climbs down and walks the square like a judge conducting a street trial. She names officers by the vice she knows: the captain who took bribes, the constable who kept a boy's secret for a bottle, the magistrate who sleeps with his servant and calls it godly mercy. She does not whisper. She names each with the weight of a sentence. The man's faces blanch as the townspeople hear things that the men did not expect to hear from another mouth.

"Prove it," one of them decries.

Paige smiles. "You're the ones who always want proof." She points to the parsonage where keys are kept loose. "Search him," she says to a baker standing in the crowd. "Find the pocketbook of his confessions."

The baker protests. The smell of danger tithes the air. But the crowd is not one voice; it is a million choices pressed close. A few lean in to pry the captain's pockets. They find a string of coins, a locket, and a folded scrap of paper. The scrap says names in a boy's hand. Women recognize humming voices in the ink. A name is heavy now. The man who has been called holy goes white.

"You see?" Paige says. "You built a machine of guilt and fed it with the hands of your own. Who will judge them if not you?"

They hesitate. It is a small victory. But TIDE is not a single victory. It is a method. She needs to escalate.

Cotton Mather arrives with robes damp and eyes like a ledger. He moves through the crowd with the luxury of a man who expects to be listened to. He opens his mouth and the town quiets because books are a kind of authority itself.

"Order," he says. "We must not let chaos masquerade as justice."

Paige watches him set his chin. He smells like glue and pages. She steps close and says, "Your books burn better than men." The words hiss like a match. Mather's face reddens. He reaches for the pommel of a whip he keeps for theatrics and finds, to his surprise, a loop of rope where it should have been.

Paige has worked quietly: ropes in stables, nails loosened on the magistrate's chairs, meat salted with the wrong spice to make men thirst. She has baited and she has lured. Tonight she does not kill quietly. She makes it simple, surgical, public.

When a magistrate orders two men to seize her, she lets them come. She stands in the center of the square, the TIDE slip hammered behind her like a banner. They run at her with clubs, righteous and ragged. She moves and takes them apart with a series of blows that are economy itself, elbow, knee, the toss of a hip. Bone cracks; men make small animal sounds and go down. The constables who try to pull their fellows away find themselves tripping over bodies and into the mud.

The crowd does not break into applause. They watch in a stunned hush, because it has always been easier to bless the plan than to watch its mechanics. To see the men fall in public is a kind of revelation and a kind of terror. The Reverend's voice becomes a thread of panic. "Seize her," he cries, "in God's name!"

Paige turns toward him and when she moves the world seems to bend. She closes the space between them in three steps. The magistrate reaches for a knife and finds instead a thick rope looped around his wrist. He tries to pull free. She pulls back and the loop slides tight. The magistrate's face, the one that once smiled at auctions and whispered to judges, goes grey. His knees hit the boards and the boards know the weight of him now. He pleads and they all hear the voice of a man who believed himself safe.

She sets her palm on his crown as if blessing, and then drives his face into the mud. "Remember your sermons," she says. "Practice them on yourself."

They hang him from the very beam he kept for others, not because they are crueler than he, but because the beam is a grammar of actions and actions speak louder than prayers. Men watch as their arbiter blinks and turns to puppet in a lesson he made himself. Someone screams. Someone laughs. The sound is so human it splits the night.

By the time dawn rides a thin horse across the horizon, nine men lie with mouths open where they once closed other mouths. The magistrates who survive walk as if they have been measured in inches and found wanting. Cotton Mather writes a sermon that smells of smoke and fear. He calls it repentance and calls for ropes to be returned to their proper owners. The town listens because order must be performed.

Paige sits on the steps of the meetinghouse, her hands black with ash from the TIDE slip, her face a map of cuts and rain. She has not avoided blood; she has taught it to speak the truth the men would not. She holds the pamphlet before her and copies its lines into her own voice until the letters are worn into her skin.

This is not the end. This is the experiment. She knows the men will retaliate with sermon and statute, with accusation and a thousand small cruelties. But she also knows that once a machine sees its reflection, it does not easily go back to pretending it was not made.

She tucks the original TIDE slip into a hollow in the meetinghouse beam where it can be found again if it must, and keeps the words in her mouth. The town will call her many things before they learn the right one. Propaganda is their name for a woman who refuses their silence.

Paige stands and looks over the square. Men sweep up blood as if it were confetti. Women hold children tight. The bell rings, a hollow sound. She lifts her hand and the gesture is small and terrible. "Read it," she says. "Then remember it."

She walks away while they read. The fold hums under her ribs. The TIDE is a weapon now, sharp and legal and terrible, and she has dressed it in the language of power. Wherever they hang a sign, she will nail a question.

In the morning, the town tells its story: the witch who taught the judges to fear themselves, the woman who made men answer for what they had done. They will alternately hate her and fear her and make her name into prayers and threats. They will call her Propaganda Paige and wear the name like a badge of caution.

She prefers the pamphlet's first line, simple and without flourish: Invert the altar, and the altar will show its bones.

She folds the TIDE into her palm and walks toward the river where men wash their hands and think themselves clean. Tonight the water will not answer them.
Tonight, it will hold the shape of what they did and give it back.

# ~6
## The Confession of Mather

Morning rises wrong. The air over Salem smells of wet ink and blood. The river runs dark with ash from the fires in the woods. The sky holds a sickly yellow at the edges, like an old bruise refusing to fade. Bells toll for repentance, but no one knows who for.

Paige stands at the edge of town and watches the smoke roll from chimneys that used to smell of bread and now smell of burnt wood and fear. The name *Propaganda Paige* has reached every corner. Children chant it to test their bravery. Men spit it into the mud to prove loyalty. Women whisper it like a psalm when no one listens.

The fires she set last night have turned the town's prayers into screams. The men hold court in daylight now, too afraid to gather by candle. They call it vigilance. They mean panic.

At the heart of it sits Cotton Mather, the architect of hysteria. His pamphlets are pinned to doors like commandments. His words are the air the men breathe before they kill. He writes of devils and virtue, of the female tongue as a serpent. He writes so the men can act without thought and still call it faith.

Paige walks toward his house as if it has been waiting for her. The parsonage stands proud and rotted, its porch sagging under the weight of sanctity. A printing press hums inside, steady as a heartbeat. Servants rush in and out with stacks of parchment. The ink smells like tar and vanity.

She waits by the door until a boy exits carrying a bundle. He nods, polite, and steps aside. Paige catches the door with her boot before it closes. She slips in silent. The house is a cathedral of paper, stacks, scrolls, manuscripts piled to the ceiling. Each page is a sermon or accusation, a written noose.

Mather sits in the center of it all like a spider in a web, his quill scratching fast, hand smeared black to the wrist. His lips move as he writes. He doesn't see her yet.

Paige watches him from the shadows. His desk is cluttered with bones, tiny ones, from birds or rats. Charms. Fetishes. He preaches against superstition and builds his own from ink and corpses.

She steps closer, and the floor creaks. He freezes. The quill hovers midair.

"Who disturbs the sanctum?" His voice is steady but tired.

Paige answers, "Someone who's read your work."

He turns, blinking, eyes sharp. "Then you know truth when you hear it."

"I know noise," she says.

He studies her, the coat, the cuts, the dirt. "So you're her. The witch with words."

"Close enough," Paige says.

He stands, slow. "You've sown chaos. You've led good men astray."

"I just gave them a mirror," she says. "They did the rest."

He circles her like a hawk. "You think yourself righteous. But your power is illusion. You twist language, you mimic holiness."

Paige steps toward the desk. "You built an empire from fear. You call it faith because it sells better."

He slams his palm on the table. "Fear keeps order!"

"Fear keeps corpses," she replies.

He laughs, short and bitter. "You think yourself a philosopher? You're a murderer."

"I've killed fewer than you have sermons."

Mather's face hardens. He points to the stacks of papers around them. "These are not weapons."

Paige picks one up. "Everything that makes a man believe he's right is a weapon." She tears it in half.

He lunges, grabbing her wrist. "Blasphemer!"

She twists free, grabs his ink bottle, and hurls it across the wall. It explodes, black running down like blood.

"You call me witch, devil, whore, words older than your spine. And every time you say them, a man feels clean enough to kill."

He straightens, breathing hard. "If my words are strong, it's because they carry God's weight."

"God's too busy burying your victims."

He sneers. "You think He listens to women?"

Paige smiles. "He's listening now."

Mather reaches for a knife hidden under his papers. She sees it glint. He swings, clumsy. She catches his wrist, twists until the blade clatters to the floor. She kicks it aside.

"Do you know why I came?" she asks.

"To tempt me," he spits.

"To teach you."

He laughs, a dry, papery sound. "You presume to teach Cotton Mather?"

She steps behind him, grabs his collar, and slams his head onto the desk. The quill snaps. He gasps. "We'll study your words," she says. "Backwards."

"What?"

"You build your power in rhythm. Sermons, spells, they're the same trick. Break the rhythm, break the hold."

She flips one of his sermons open. "Let's read."

He struggles, but she holds him down. "Say it," she commands.

"The light… drives out…" he starts.

"Backwards," she says.

He hesitates. "Out drives light the…"

"Louder."

He obeys, the words clumsy and ugly in reverse. "Out drives light the…"

"Keep going."

He stumbles through lines, voice shaking. The syllables warp, the meaning collapsing. His theology turns to nonsense. Sweat beads on his brow.

Paige's grip tightens. "Feel it? That's your God choking on your syntax."

He snarls, "You're insane."

"No," she says. "You are, you just wrote it better."

She shoves him aside and starts tearing pages, one after another. Ink dust fills the air. "Every sermon you ever wrote is a death sentence disguised as devotion."

He crawls toward the fallen knife. She steps on his hand. "Confess," she says.

"I have nothing to confess."

"You have everything."

She leans down. "Say it. Say you made this up."

He winces. "It's not a lie."

"Then it's worse, it's marketing."

He groans, twisting under her boot. "I did what I must. To save them."

"Save who?"

"The innocent."

"There are none left," she says. "You burned them."

He glares up. "And what are you? A savior?"

"No," she says softly. "A correction."

She lifts her boot. He grabs the knife again, lunging upward. She sidesteps and drives her knee into his chest. The knife falls. She catches it and presses the point to his throat.

"You believe in confession?"

He nods, barely breathing.

"Then confess."

His lips tremble. "I… was wrong."

"Not enough." She presses harder. "Say it like a sermon."

His voice cracks. "I was wrong! I made monsters and called them saints!"

"Better," she says.

He gasps, "God forgive me."

"Ask them," she says.

"Who?"

"The women you killed."

He shakes his head. "They're gone."

She leans closer. "They're listening."

He sobs. "I did it for belief."

"You did it for applause."

She pulls the blade away, tosses it onto the desk. "Keep talking."

He collapses forward, sobbing, the ink from the desk staining his face like a priest's ash. "I saw demons everywhere," he whispers. "And they all looked like women."

Paige crouches beside him. "That's the trick. You made women the mirror of your fear so you'd never have to face yourself."

He looks up, eyes wild. "What are you then?"

She stands. "The mirror you avoided."

He laughs, broken, shaking. "Then show me."

She takes one of his half-written pamphlets, still wet, and presses it against his face. "Read," she says.

He wheezes, "I can't see."

"Exactly."

She holds it there until he chokes on the ink, the words seeping into his skin. "That's how your faith works," she says. "Blind and full of paper."

He coughs, trembling. "Kill me."

She steps back. "No. You'll print your confession."

He blinks, stunned. "What?"

"Every press in this town spreads your lies. You'll use them to spread truth."

He stares at her. "They'll never believe me."

"They believed you before."

He nods slowly, broken. "And if I refuse?"

She looks at the press. "Then it prints your blood."

He believes her.

Paige turns to the machine, wipes her hands, and begins feeding paper into the rollers. "Write it," she says.

His hands shake as he dips the quill in ink. "What do I say?"

"The truth," she says. "Say that fear and virtue are the same trade. Say you sold both."

He writes, each stroke a tremor. The page fills with black. When he finishes, she reads it aloud.

"I, Cotton Mather, do confess that I have mistaken judgment for faith, that I have named women devils to excuse the evil in men, that I have written of purity to hide desire, and that I have mistaken power for grace. I am the architect of hysteria, the author of pain. I am not chosen. I am guilty."

She nods. "Good."

He stares at it. "You'll hang me for this."

"I'll print you," she says.

She takes the sheet and places it in the press. The gears turn. The ink bites the page. She pulls it out, holds it to the candlelight. "Now you've written something worth keeping."

He slumps back in his chair, drained. "They'll kill me."

"They'll thank you first," she says.

Paige gathers the printed confession, folds it, and tucks it into her coat. "When the town wakes, they'll find this on every door."

He closes his eyes. "And you?"

She pauses. "I'll keep writing."

He opens one eye, faintly smiling. "You sound like me."

She looks at him. "No. I sound like consequence."

She leaves him there, hands black with ink, face lit by the dying candle. Outside, dawn scrapes the rooftops. The streets are empty but not quiet; every building hums with dread. Paige moves fast, posting the confessions on doors, on the church gate, on the scaffold.

By noon, the whole town has read it. Men tear the pages down, shouting forgery. Women hide copies under bread cloths. Children memorize the words and whisper them in alleyways.

Cotton Mather sits alone in his study. The press still turns. He can't stop it. Each page rolls out another copy of his confession, his own handwriting made infinite. He tries to smash it, but the gears lock, the iron arm catching his sleeve. He struggles, screams, pulls, and the machine takes his hand, grinding flesh into pulp. The sound is awful. The ink turns red.

When Paige returns at dusk, she finds him slumped beside it, eyes open, blood on the pages. The press keeps working, one mangled hand still wedged in the mechanism.

She watches the pages slide out, one after another printed in red, half blood, half ink.

She takes one and reads the words again. "I am not chosen. I am guilty."

Paige folds the page carefully, slips it into her coat. "That's enough theology for one century," she says.

She turns to leave, but stops at the door. "You wanted to save souls," she says quietly. "Now you've saved one, yours."

She steps into the rain.

By morning, the press will still run. The servants will find the house red with ink. The men will call it witchcraft. The women will call it justice. The children will start to rhyme the confession as if it were a prayer.

And in the burned fields outside Salem, the wind will scatter scraps of the confession through the grass like scripture lost to time.

Paige walks through it, coat open, the TIDE Manifesto folded at her chest. The river catches the papers one by one, carrying them downstream toward the sea.

# ~7
# The River Ritual

Rain the color of steel needles stings the earth. The river groans under it, swollen and angry, turning the mud path into a bleeding vein that leads straight into the heart of Salem. It is midnight, and every torch looks afraid to burn.

Reverend Parris limps toward the river with a Bible in one hand and a pistol in the other. His bandaged face gleams under the torchlight like a rotten apple polished for judgment day. Around him: a dozen men, drunk on fear and holy purpose. Behind them: the wives, the watchers, the whisperers.

"Bring the witch to the water!" Parris bellows. "Let the river taste her sin!"

The crowd answers with a noise that's not quite cheering — more like the sound a wound makes when you press it too hard.

They don't see her yet. But she sees them.

Paige is already standing at the river's edge, coat soaked, rope coiled at her hip, eyes shining like flint. The current slaps at her boots. She looks calm, almost reverent. The water moves the way crowds do before they riot.

"You boys brought enough rope for everyone?" she calls.

Muskets lift. Torches flare. Every man looks to Parris for the cue.

He steps forward, chest heaving. "Your time's up, witch."

She smiles. "Good news. So's yours."

Lightning hits the river. The flash turns them all white for half a heartbeat, statues in a painting of their own execution.

Then Paige moves.

She doesn't run. She strides through the current, fast and sure. A musket fires, the ball tears through her coat and into the water. Another shot, another miss. The men panic, reloading with trembling hands. Paige reaches the first man before he finishes the ramrod. She grabs his musket by the barrel and smashes it across his face. Teeth scatter like wet dice.

The next one lunges with a bayonet. She sidesteps, grabs his arm, snaps the elbow backward, and lets the blade finish its owner. He drops, gurgling.

Parris shouts scripture, voice breaking. "The Lord rebuke thee—"

Paige throws the bloody musket into the river. "He already did."

Two more charge from the bank. She meets them halfway. One swings a torch. She ducks, grabs the burning head, and shoves it into his chest. The fire eats the oil on his coat. He screams, turns into a lantern, stumbles backward into the water, and the river puts him out hard.

The second man hesitates. Paige grabs him by the collar, jerks him forward, headbutts him once. The sound is dull and final.

The crowd recoils. They've seen hangings. They've never seen a sermon this honest.

"Kill her!" Parris howls. "Kill her in His name!"

"Which one?" Paige asks.

He fires the pistol. The shot grazes her shoulder, spinning her halfway. She turns back, bleeding, grinning. "You missed your miracle."

She walks straight at him. The pistol shakes. He fires again. Click, empty. Paige's hand flashes out, knocks the weapon away, and drives her knee into his gut. He folds. She grabs the back of his neck and forces him into the water.

"Say it," she hisses. "Say you baptized women in blood."

He thrashes. "I— I cast out demons!"

"Look around." She dunks him again. "You cast out neighbors."

The river hisses over his face. When she pulls him up, he gasps, sputtering mud.

"This isn't salvation," he croaks.

"No," she says, shoving him under again. "It's education."

The men rush her, shouting, sliding in mud, swinging torches like clubs. She turns with the flow, kicks, punches, elbows, fast and ugly. One torch goes flying, lands on the bank, catches a wagon of hay. Fire roars to life, red against the rain.

Paige drags Parris upright, drenched and coughing. "This river's honest," she says. "It gives back exactly what you feed it."

He swings wildly. She lets him hit her. Then she catches his hand, twists it, and breaks the finger that used to point at witches. He howls. She shoves him down again, harder this time.

"Baptized enough?" she says.

The men freeze. They've seen her take on six, maybe ten. They're not sure how many are left breathing. They want to believe she's human, but she's moving like a rumor that forgot it wasn't real.

Ruth Parris steps out from the line of women. Her shawl is gone. Her hair clings to her face. She walks straight into the water.

"Ruth," the preacher gasps, spitting river. "Go back."

"No."

Her voice cuts through everything, rain, fire, thunder, screaming. She looks at Paige. "He told them this river washes sin."

Paige nods. "Let's see."

Ruth takes the rope from Paige's shoulder. It's the same rope that once held a girl named Mary. She loops one end around her husband's wrist, the other around a half-buried post. "You said this purifies," she says. "Don't stop now."

"Woman, obey!" he cries.

"I am," she says, and kicks his legs out. The current grabs him and slaps him against the rock. The rope holds. He thrashes, sputtering prayers that dissolve into bubbles.

One of the men charges at Ruth with a knife. Paige intercepts him, grabs his wrist, drives her boot into his knee, twists, and stabs him with his own blade. He falls screaming into the current. The river takes him without complaint.

"Anyone else need saving?" Paige shouts.

No one answers. Thunder cracks right over them. The sky lights up again, showing a field of faces, wet, pale, terrified, thinking too hard. The women on the bank stop pretending to cry. Some nod. One starts laughing, sharp and small.

Paige turns back to Parris. He's still alive, barely, face blue-white, rope cutting into his wrist. She grabs him by the chin, hauls him up enough to meet her eyes. "Say it," she says. "Say you made them kill to make you feel holy."

"I— I—"

"Louder."

"I made them kill!" he screams.

She lets him go. The river drags him down, spins him once, spits him onto the bank like trash that refused to stay buried. He lies there coughing, broken but breathing.

Paige looks at Ruth. "He'll live," she says. "Long enough to watch everything fall apart."

Ruth nods. "Then let him."

The militia on the far hill starts down, shouting, waving torches. Paige turns to meet them, breath steady. "Here comes the encore."

They fire, three, four shots, smoke and sparks. One ball tears past her ear, another punches through her sleeve.  She walks into the gunfire like it's rain.  When she reaches the first shooter, she slams the butt of his musket into his throat.  He drops.  She takes the weapon, fires point-blank into the next man's chest.  He folds like wet paper.

The others backpedal, tripping on their own courage.

Ruth steps up beside her.  "What now?"

Paige reloads the musket.  "Now they learn what a sermon sounds like when a woman writes it."

She fires into the air.  The echo rolls across the valley like thunder learning to swear.

"You built a church out of women's bones!" she shouts.  "You prayed into their mouths and called it order!"

Another shot, one man in the shoulder.  "You think holiness means hiding from the mirror? I am the mirror!"

She drops the musket, grabs a fallen man's knife, and hurls it into the torch wagon.  It bursts into flames.  The light paints the river red.

"Target," she says, voice
rising.  "Inspire.  Disrupt.  Empower."

Each word hits like a drum.  The women repeat
it.  First one, then five, then fifty voices.  The sound is

low, rough,
unstoppable. *Target. Inspire. Disrupt. Empower.*

The men fall back. The rain starts again, hard and
cleansing.

Paige turns to Ruth. "He'll write new scripture
tomorrow. That's what they do. But you've already
read the better one."

Ruth looks at her husband, broken, gasping, afraid to
move. She looks back at Paige. "What do I do now?"

Paige says, "You live like the trial never happened."

Ruth nods once. "That'll terrify them."

"Good," Paige says. "Keep it up."

She slings the rope across her shoulder, bloodied and
heavy, and starts walking downstream. The water
glows with reflected fire. The women follow her gaze as
she disappears into the dark. Behind them, men kneel
in mud they can't tell from blood, praying to a God
who isn't answering tonight.

When the river calms, bodies float where prayers used
to. Smoke curls from the torches. Ruth stands at the
edge of the water, face lit by flame, and whispers the
four words again under her breath.

Target. Inspire. Disrupt. Empower. Paige doesn't look
back.

# ~8
## The Witch's Parliament

Morning arrives gray and swollen. The storm has left the streets veined with water and the church bells do not ring. The town smells of smoke and wet rope. What was faith last night is silence today. Salem is a wound trying to remember its shape.

Paige walks through it slow, boots cutting tracks through puddles that reflect the broken steeple. The river still murmurs behind her, patient and wide, carrying scraps of burnt pages downstream. The air tastes like iron.

Men hide behind shutters. The brave ones step outside and call it inspection. Their muskets are damp and their eyes are hunted. The women move quietly, sleeves rolled, faces blank, sweeping the blood away from the meetinghouse steps. There are no trials today. There is only aftermath.

She moves among them like a shadow that knows its name. A child watches her pass, mouth open, then whispers to his mother. The mother hushes him, but her hand finds his shoulder and holds it tight.

At the door of the meetinghouse, a woman stands waiting. Ruth Parris. Hair unbound, eyes hollow but steady. Her voice is hoarse when she speaks. "They left him in the rectory. Breathing. But not preaching."

Paige nods. "Then the river did what sermons never could."

"They will come for you," Ruth says.

"They already did."

Ruth steps aside. "Then come inside. We're not finished."

The meetinghouse smells of old smoke and new purpose. Candles flicker in tin holders. The pews have been pushed aside. Thirty women stand or sit on the floor. Some cradle infants. Some carry bruises. All of them look up when Paige enters.

They do not bow. They do not cross themselves. They just watch.

Ruth closes the door and bars it. "This is what's left," she says. "The widows. The accused. The forgotten. We've decided we're done waiting for rescue."

Paige looks at the faces. "Then why call me?"

"Because you started something," Ruth says. "We need to know how to finish it."

A woman in the corner speaks, voice shaking. "They will hang us for this."

Paige meets her eyes. "They already hung you. You just haven't noticed yet."

A ripple of laughter breaks out, half fear, half relief.

Ruth takes a candle from the table and sets it in the center of the room. "We're calling it a parliament," she says. "They call it witchcraft. So be it. Let's talk."

Paige stands near the flame. "Talk is what built the gallows. Maybe it can tear it down."

The women draw closer. The light touches their faces one by one, turning them into a gallery of different kinds of courage.

An old midwife speaks first. "They took my daughter for healing a fever. Said herbs were spells. Said her touch was sin. Now she's in the ground. I want justice."

A younger woman with a scar on her cheek adds, "They took my husband for listening. They said he doubted the court. They made me watch them whip him."

Another whispers, "They burned my field. Said my cows gave sour milk because I cursed them. I had to dig my own grave and then they changed their minds. They laughed."

The room fills with stories until the air trembles with them. Pain becomes a kind of music. Paige lets them speak until there are no more words left, only the sound of breath and the drip of wax.

Then she says, "What they fear most is that you will speak the same language. They kept you apart because they know what happens when women start comparing notes."

Ruth nods. "So what do we do?"

Paige walks to the pulpit. The wood is charred but standing. She puts her hand on it like she is swearing an oath. "You build a new scripture."

Murmurs move through the room.

She says, "There was a pamphlet once, hidden under the church. The Theocratic Inversion Doctrine Experiment. They called it TIDE. It was written by someone who wanted to test the judges the way they tested others. I used it to turn their own sermons against them. But it's not enough. It's too careful. Too clever. It needs to be rewritten."

Ruth steps forward. "By whom?"

Paige looks around the room. "By you."

The old midwife frowns. "We can't write."

"Then speak. I'll write it for you."

Paige drags a table to the center and sets a sheet of parchment on it. The candle throws shadows that look like wings. She dips a quill in the ink. "Tell me what needs to live."

The midwife speaks first. "We want the trials to end."

Paige writes, the quill scratching like firewood catching flame.

The woman with the scar says, "We want our names back."

Paige writes again. A farmer's widow says, "We want land. Not borrowed, not stolen. Ours."

Paige writes slower now. "That's the first real blasphemy I've heard all night."

Ruth says, "We want to decide who speaks for God. Maybe no one."

Paige looks up. "That's the second."

More voices rise. "We want the right to work." "We want the right to say no." "We want the right to fight back."

The words layer like bricks. The room gets hotter. The women are standing now, shoulders touching, eyes alive.

Paige writes until the ink stains her fingers. When the parchment is full, she flips it and keeps going. The words come faster than thought. The ink runs. The air smells like blood again, but no one minds.

Finally she sets the quill down. "Read it," Ruth says.

Paige lifts the sheet and reads aloud. Her voice fills the room like a storm taking shape.

"We, the women of Salem, being sick of silence, do declare that fear is not virtue, that obedience is not purity, that the voice of God does not sound like a man's throat clearing. We name our daughters not for saints but for survivors. We bury no more innocents to feed the vanity of judges. We reclaim the word witch as one who knows and one who heals. We speak the new creed of TIDE: Target. Inspire. Disrupt. Empower."

The room goes still. Paige lowers the parchment. "That's what it says now."

Ruth repeats it, slow. "Target. Inspire. Disrupt. Empower."

A woman in the back whispers it. Another joins. Then another. The sound grows until it's a chant. The walls seem to lean closer to listen. Paige stands among them, quiet. The words are not hers anymore. That's the point.

Ruth steps to the window and pulls the curtain aside. The square outside is empty. Smoke from the burned wagons still hangs in the air. "They will come for us when they hear this."

Paige nods. "Then make sure they hear it loud."

The midwife moves to the door. "What do we do when they knock?"

Paige smiles faintly. "Ask them what they're afraid of. Then show them."

The door rattles as if on cue. A man's voice outside shouts, "By order of the magistrate, this meeting is unlawful!"

The women look at one another. Fear flickers, then hardens into resolve.

Ruth says, "We're in session."

Paige takes a step toward the door. "Let them in."

The latch lifts. The door opens. Three constables stand there, wet and angry. One holds a pistol, one a rope, one a warrant. They stop when they see the women lined up like a jury that already knows the verdict.

Paige says, "You're late."

The man with the pistol stammers. "We— we're here to disperse this—"

"This what?" Ruth asks.

"This heresy."

Paige walks up to him until the pistol presses her coat. "Then shoot the first heretic. Show them what justice looks like today."
He hesitates.

The midwife says, "Go on."

The women close in, shoulder to shoulder, eyes burning. The pistol trembles.

Paige takes it from his hand, slow, calm. "You forgot your faith," she says, and brings the butt of it down on his temple. He drops. The other two reach for her, and the room explodes into motion.

Candles fall. Tables crash. Women shout and swing. The air fills with smoke and fury. Paige moves through it like she's been waiting her whole life. A rope flies toward her; she catches it and loops it around the nearest man's arm, jerks hard, and sends him into a wall. The last one raises his club. Ruth smashes a candlestick into his mouth. Teeth scatter. He falls without drama.

When it's over, the floor is a mess of blood and wax. The parchment lies in the corner, edges singed. Ruth picks it up and holds it high. "This is the law now."

The women cheer, not loud, but sure.

Paige kneels beside the man she hit. He's breathing. She wipes her hand on his coat and stands. "Take their weapons," she says. "Burn the warrant. Keep the rope."

Ruth does as told. The midwife ties the rope into a knot and hangs it over the pulpit like a relic. "We'll remember," she says.
Paige looks at the women. "The next time they come, they'll bring fire."

"Then we meet at night," Ruth says.

"In the woods," says the woman with the scar.

"By the river," says another.

Paige nods. "Then it's settled."

She walks to the door and steps into the cold morning. The town is waking, uneasy. Somewhere a bell starts to ring but falters halfway through. She looks up at the church steeple and sees men moving inside, silhouettes against the smoke.

Ruth joins her. "What do we call ourselves?" she asks.

Paige looks at the sky, pale and wet, then at the river beyond the trees. "Call yourselves the storm," she says.

The women file out behind them. They carry nothing but the parchment and the blood on their sleeves. They move through the square, silent, a procession of heretics with clean hands. Men stare from doorways but do not stop them. The town feels smaller in their wake.

At the edge of the river, they stop. Paige takes the parchment and holds it above the water. "This is not for the priests," she says. "This is for whoever comes next." She lets it go. The current takes it, unrolling it like a prayer. The ink bleeds, but the words remain visible as it drifts away.
Ruth watches it float toward the horizon. "Will they remember?"

Paige answers, "They always do, eventually. Fear just delays it."

The women stay there until the parchment disappears around the bend. Then one by one they kneel and touch the water, not in worship, but in promise.

Paige turns back toward the town. Smoke rises again from somewhere near the square. Voices carry on the wind, angry, afraid, confused. She knows what comes next. Salem will try to rebuild its lie. But the lie has cracks now, and the cracks have names.

Ruth says, "What if they burn us?"

Paige smiles. "Then they'll light their own pyres. You can't burn what's already fire."

The wind lifts her hair. The sky clears a little, enough to show a sliver of sun. The river glitters like a blade. The women begin to walk, spreading out toward their homes, their fields, their ghosts. The chant follows them like a heartbeat.

Target. Inspire. Disrupt. Empower. Paige stays last. She watches the water swallow the sun and whispers, "You started it. I just finished the translation."

When she finally turns away, the town feels smaller and the century feels closer. Somewhere a baby cries, and a rooster crows as if to mark a new kind of morning.

The Witch's Parliament is adjourned.

# ~9
# The Flood

The rain does not fall. It attacks.

Sheets of it hammer the rooftops until shingles lift like scales. The streets turn to veins of brown water pulsing through the town. The river has left its bed and come to reclaim its worshippers.

Paige stands in the square. Her coat clings to her like armor made of ghosts. Water climbs her boots and tries to drag her toward the gallows. The ropes above sway, empty, as if waiting to decide who deserves to hang next.

The bell in the steeple tolls once. Then again. Then stops. The sound drowns in the storm.

Across the square, Reverend Parris staggers from the church. His face is gray, his robes soaked. He clutches his Bible to his chest like it's a weapon. Behind him, Cotton Mather limps, arm bound in cloth, eyes hollow. The magistrate follows, holding a torn paper decree that the rain has already erased.

Paige watches them wade into the square like rats fleeing a ship.

"This is judgment," the magistrate shouts. "The Lord drowns the wicked first."

Paige looks at the sky. "Then you should start swimming."

A gust of wind steals his hat. The crowd laughs before it remembers to be afraid.

Ruth appears beside Paige, soaked to the bone, hair plastered to her cheeks.

"They say the storm is punishment for the parliament," she says.

Paige nods. "Then it's working."

The magistrate raises his hand. "Seize her!"

No one moves. The water is already past their ankles. The current pulls at their feet like a whisper saying no.

Paige steps forward until she stands knee-deep. "This is not your flood," she says. "This is the world cleaning itself."

Lightning flashes. The church steeple glows white, then black again. In that split second the faces of the men look carved from wax. The women look carved from stone.

Ruth lifts her chin. "Target."

The women scattered around the square answer her. "Inspire. Disrupt. Empower."

Their voices rise and mix with thunder.

The magistrate's lip curls. "You mock God."

Paige smiles. "I mirror Him."

He charges. He has a sword now, ceremonial, useless, heavy. Paige meets him halfway. The blade slides across her coat and misses flesh. She grabs his wrist, twists, and the sword clatters into the water. She elbows his throat, shoves him backward, and lets the river take him. His scream cuts short when he swallows the current.

Mather flinches. "Stop this madness!"

Paige turns to him. "You built it."

He tries to raise a hand in blessing. The bound arm won't lift. The other shakes. "Repent," he gasps.

"I did," she says. "I repented of silence."

Two constables rush her. One with a musket, one with a chain. She steps between them. The musket fires into the air. She catches the chain, loops it once around the shooter's neck, and pulls. The second tries to cut her loose. She drives her knee into his gut and drops him face-first into the flood. When she releases the chain, the first man doesn't stand again.

The townspeople scream. The water swallows half the sound.

Ruth grabs a torch from the gutter. It hisses but holds flame. She throws it onto the church steps. The oil from the lamps catches. Fire blooms red against the rain.

"This is not the Lord's fire," Parris shouts from behind the smoke.

"No," Paige says. "It's yours. I'm just returning it."

She walks toward him through waist-deep water. He backs away until the current lifts his robe. His Bible slips from his hand and drifts between them.

"You cannot kill me," he says. "I am His messenger."

Paige picks up the Bible, heavy and soaked. "Then He should have chosen better paper." She throws it back at him. It hits his chest like a stone.

"Confess," she says.

He shakes his head. "Never."

She reaches him, grips the front of his robe, and drags him forward. "You preached mercy while drowning girls. You called it faith. I call it arithmetic."

She pushes him under. The water swallows his shout. When she lets him up, he coughs mud.

"Say it," she says.

He gasps. "I—"

"Say you knew."

He nods once. "I knew."

She releases him. He falls back into the water and floats, eyes open, lips moving soundlessly as if praying to something that has stopped listening.

Behind her, the square has turned to chaos. Men slip on cobbles. Women wade forward, pulling down banners from the church wall, tearing them into strips. The midwife ties them into a long rope. The scarred wife loops it around the statue of a judge and pulls until it topples into the flood. Stone cracks. The head sinks.

Paige watches it disappear. "Now it's balanced," she says.

Lightning again. The storm lights every face in silver and black. The water has reached the gallows. The ropes sway and twist. One breaks loose and floats down toward the women. Ruth grabs it, coils it over her shoulder like inheritance.

The old midwife points at the men still holding ground by the steps. "They will come again," she says.

Paige nods. "Then we meet them here."

Mather wades closer, shaking. "This is not victory," he says. "This is damnation."

Paige turns. "You confuse the two because you've never seen justice done sober."

He tries to speak again. She touches his mouth with two fingers. "Silence is the only clean word you know. Keep it."

He trembles and steps back, eyes wild, as if the flood itself were taking instruction from her.

Ruth climbs the gallows stairs. Water laps at the first rung. She raises the rope high. "For every woman they drowned," she calls, "let the river take one of theirs."

The women answer her with a single sharp cry that sounds like thunder breaking its chain. They move as one. They drag the wounded men from the steps and shove them into the deep. Some fight. Some pray. The river treats both the same.

Paige does not stop them. She only watches. The current writes dark circles around each body before claiming it. One by one, the shouts fade into the storm.

When the last is gone, silence lands like snow. The fire on the church steps flickers and goes out. The square steams.

Ruth lowers the rope. "Is it finished?"

Paige looks around. "Nothing finishes. It only changes shape."

The women stand in the rising water, breathing hard. The town is half gone now. The river has claimed streets and fences and memory. What remains stands clean and raw.

Paige steps up onto the gallows beside Ruth. The beam creaks. The water swirls below like liquid glass.

"This is your scripture now," she says. "The flood is not punishment. It's instruction. Build again, but not like before."

Ruth nods. "And if they come?"

"Then you already know the sermon."

The wind turns cold. It tears at their clothes, drives the smoke toward the forest. The first pale light of morning slips through the clouds. The rain slows. The sound of the river fades to a steady heartbeat.

Bodies float by in twos and threes. The current carries them toward the sea. The water glints red around them but clears quickly. It takes what it wants and moves on.

Paige steps down. She walks to the ruined courthouse door and nails a single page to the frame. It is the TIDE Manifesto, smeared but legible. The ink has bled into the paper like veins. It reads:

*We, the women of Salem, name ourselves free. We will not feed fear again. We are the storm, not its casualty.*

She hammers it until the wood splits, then turns. The women watch her in silence. The sound of dripping fills the air like applause held in breath.

Paige walks through the square. The water parts for her knees. The sky above breaks open and a shaft of light falls on the gallows beam. For the first time in months, the sun touches Salem.

She stops at the edge of the river. Ruth joins her.

"What will you do now?" Ruth asks.

Paige looks west where the horizon flickers between cloud and gold. "There's another hunt waiting. They'll call it enlightenment this time."

Ruth laughs once, low and tired. "Will you go?"

Paige nods. "Someone has to make sure the light burns the right people."

She steps into the current. It climbs her waist, her chest, her throat. For a moment it looks like she might vanish. Then the water calms, and she is gone.

The river smooths its back as if sealing the story. The women stand on the bank, watching. Behind them, the town begins to creak and shift. Doors open. Children crawl from hiding. The bell tower leans but holds.

Ruth turns to the others. "She's not gone," she says. "She's just moving."

The midwife nods. "Like weather."

They walk from the square, water dripping from their skirts. The chant rises again, quieter now but certain.

Target. Inspire. Disrupt. Empower.

Paige's rope floats downstream, caught on a branch, glistening like gold. The clouds thin. The sun opens its eye wider. The town breathes. The river hums a single note that sounds almost like peace.

And the world, for one clean second, forgets to lie.

# ~10
## Fold to the Next Hunt

Morning broke over Salem like an exhausted confession. The storm had spent itself, but the sky still looked bruised. The air was thick with the smell of wet ash and river mud. Every plank, every brick, every tool left in the street seemed to carry the memory of violence. The gallows was half collapsed, its beam split, its rope missing. The town was quiet in the way that comes after screaming, not peace, but shock pretending to be prayer.

Paige stood in the middle of the square, her boots sinking into mud that used to be a street. Her coat was torn, her hair hung heavy against her neck, and her face was calm. Ruth stood beside her, shoulders squared, eyes fixed on the courthouse where the TIDE Manifesto still hung nailed to the door. The ink had bled, but the words were alive. The page fluttered like a heartbeat.

"It's over," Ruth said softly.

Paige shook her head. "Nothing's ever over. It just changes costume."

The door of the church creaked open. Three men stepped out, each dressed in the rags of authority. The first held a pistol, the second a Bible, the third a rope with a noose tied at the end. They had washed the blood from their collars, but not from their eyes. They saw her and froze. The pistol wavered. The man behind it licked his lips.

"You'll hang for this," he said, trying to sound official. The sound came out thin.

Paige took a step forward. The mud swallowed the sound of her boots. "Try," she said.

The man raised his gun. His hands shook. The shot cracked the air and hit the courthouse wall, breaking a piece of stone. Before the smoke cleared, she was on him. She wrenched the pistol from his grip, swung it like a hammer, and smashed his teeth in one clean strike. Blood sprayed the mud. He went down choking on it.

The second man raised the Bible like it could shield him. "Repent!" he cried.

She snatched it from his hands and slammed it into his face. The leather cover broke his nose. He dropped to his knees, blood dripping onto the pages. She flipped the book open. The ink had run from the flood, leaving blank pages. She dropped it beside him. "Looks like your god lost his script."

The third man hesitated. The noose dangled from his hand. He turned to run. Paige let him. "Go," she said. "Live long enough to remember what you saw."

He didn't look back. He ran toward the river and disappeared behind the fog.

Ruth stepped forward. "You could have killed all three."

Paige looked down at the bodies. "I did. Some people just take longer to die."

They turned toward the courthouse. The door hung open, and the TIDE Manifesto still held to the frame. Ruth touched the page with her fingertips. "Will it last?"

Paige nodded. "It doesn't need to. It just needs to spread."

The wind shifted. Horses. The sound came from the east road, slow, deliberate, armored. Six riders emerged from the mist, each wearing black coats slick with rain, rifles across their saddles. Their faces were pale and angry, men sent to clean up what they didn't understand. Their leader, tall and thin, raised a hand. The others stopped.

"Who commands this town?" he called.

Paige stepped into the open. "I do."

He squinted. "Your name?"

"Propaganda Paige."

The man laughed. "So the stories are true. The witch who drowned a town."

She smiled. "I prefer teacher."

He raised his rifle. "I prefer executioner."

"Everyone needs a hobby."

He gave the order. "Take her."

The riders moved fast. Mud sprayed from their hooves as they spread out. Paige didn't wait. She ran straight toward them, pulling the knife from her belt. The first rider swung a rifle like a club. She ducked under it, slashed his thigh, and pulled him from the saddle. He hit the ground hard. She turned, caught his rifle as it fell, and fired point-blank into the chest of the second man before his horse even stopped moving. The blast blew him back into the mud.

The others charged. Ruth grabbed a pistol from the dead man's belt and took cover behind the gallows beam. The shot cracked loud and clean, hitting one of the riders square in the shoulder. He spun, lost his grip, and tumbled into the water pooling at the base of the square.

Paige was already moving. She ducked another swing, rolled beneath a horse's legs, and came up behind the rider. She grabbed his coat, yanked him backward, and drove the knife under his jaw. His body went stiff, then loose. She pushed him off and took the reins of his horse.

The leader reloaded his rifle and aimed. He fired once. The shot grazed her arm, cutting fabric and skin. She didn't flinch. She spurred the horse forward, closing the distance before he could reload. She threw herself from the saddle and hit him square in the chest. The rifle flew from his hands. They hit the ground together. He tried to reach for a knife. She broke his wrist, took the blade, and jammed it through his throat.

The last rider turned to run. Ruth shouted, "Paige!" and threw her the pistol. Paige caught it midair, spun, and fired once. The bullet hit the man in the spine. He pitched forward and hit the mud face-first. The horse bolted into the trees.

The square was silent again, except for the horses snorting and the hiss of rain returning. The air smelled of powder and metal. Paige wiped blood from her cheek with the back of her hand. Ruth lowered her pistol and stepped beside her.

"You're bleeding," Ruth said.

"So is Salem."

The women of the parliament began to emerge from the shadows, the midwife with her rope, the scarred wife with her iron skillet, the girl with the long braid holding a knife too big for her hands. They looked at the bodies, then at Paige. There was no fear in their eyes. Only certainty.

"Bury them deep," Paige said. "We don't need ghosts with uniforms."

They nodded. They would dig. They would salt the ground. They would make sure nothing planted here grew the same again.

From the courthouse steps, Cotton Mather appeared, one arm bound tight to his chest. His face was pale, eyes sunken. He held a single broadside in his good hand, his confession, copied through the night. The ink had run pink in places, mixed with rain and blood. He looked at Paige like a man who had learned the shape of regret too late.

"I will print it," he said. "Until the ink runs out."

"Then use your blood," Paige said. "It's darker."

He nodded once. He might have meant it.

Behind him, Reverend Parris watched from the church doorway. His collar was stained, his Bible gone. For once, his mouth didn't move. He had no sermon left to sell. Paige met his eyes. "This is your gospel now," she said. "Learn to read it."

Ruth came to her side. "What happens next?"

Paige looked east, where the mist was beginning to burn away. "I leave."

Ruth frowned. "And us?"

"You stay. Feed the living. Bury the dead with names. Keep the fire small and steady."

"And if they come again?"

Paige smiled. "Then make them wish they hadn't."

She started toward the river. The water had gone down, but it still moved fast, carrying broken wood and the memory of last night's screams. The current hissed against the rocks like it was whispering her name. The fold was waiting. She could feel it, humming beneath the surface, a seam in the world begging to be opened.

A sound broke behind her, the sharp snap of a musket being cocked. She turned. A man limped from the alley, his face half burned, one arm bound in rags. He was one of the riders she hadn't finished. He raised his rifle with his good arm and spat blood into the dirt.

"You think you're salvation," he said. "You're just another curse."

Paige took a slow step forward. "You might be right."

He fired. The shot went wide. She didn't blink. She crossed the distance between them in three steps, caught the barrel, and shoved it into his chest. His finger twitched, and the gun fired again. The smoke blew between them. He looked down, saw the hole, and started to fall. She grabbed his collar, held him upright, and whispered in his ear.

"God was not here tonight."

She let him drop. His body hit the mud with a sound that barely mattered.

Ruth was watching from the edge of the square. "You didn't have to."

"Yes, I did."

She wiped her knife clean on his coat and walked to the riverbank. The water glistened with thin sunlight, black and gold, alive again. She turned back once. Ruth stood with the women. The Manifesto fluttered in the wind. Children were gathering around it, pointing at the letters they could not yet read. They would learn.

Paige smiled. "Tomorrow they'll tell each other that God was here."

Ruth heard her and nodded. "And?"

"He wasn't," Paige said. "I was."

The women bowed their heads. Not in worship. In respect.

Paige stepped into the water. The current reached her knees, her waist, her chest. The fold shimmered ahead of her like a curtain made of heat. She reached out. The air split open. Light poured through. It smelled like wet stone and fire and ink. On the other side she saw marble halls, silk gowns, and powdered men writing liberty with one hand and hiding chains with the other. She saw guillotines polished with philosophy. She saw the next lie wearing reason's face.

She laughed softly. "The Enlightenment," she said. "Let's see what burns."

She looked back at Ruth one last time. The rope hung from her shoulder like a relic. The women stood behind her, still as a wall. The men watched from doorways, too afraid to move. For once, that was the right kind of fear.

Paige stepped into the light. The fold closed behind her like a breath being held.

The river stilled. The wind eased. Salem stood in its new silence.

Ruth turned to the women. "Work," she said simply.

They did. They dragged the bodies. They patched the roofs. They gathered children and told them the truth. Cotton Mather set up his press and began printing again, this time with a trembling hand. Parris stood outside his church and kept his mouth shut. The bell in the steeple leaned but didn't fall. The town began, for the first time, to live.

Downstream, a single scrap of parchment drifted against a root. The ink had run, but the words were still there.

*We are the storm. Not its casualty.*

The river carried it on, whispering her name.

## About EATMS Productions

What's happening to women now is not random. It's structural.

Policy, culture, technology, and power are moving in the same direction.

EATMS maps them clearly and shows how to respond.

This title is part of an ongoing body of work. All EATMS Productions titles, across all series, authors, and formats, are components of a single connected project.

Start here: EATMS System Primer — Free Bundle
https://eatms.gumroad.com/l/dyvzbw

For full catalog or inquiries: eatms.me

Free survival booklet + EATMS updates: email "EATMS" to eatms@pm.me

*Please feel free to burn part or all of this book, safely, as an effigy.*

www.ingramcontent.com/pod-product-compliance
Lightning Source LLC
Chambersburg PA
CBHW030134260626
47156CB00008B/2938